Lavinia
and the
Magic
Ring

Thank you for the inspiration to:
Andersen for the match girl, Tolkien for the
ring, King for the stare, Voltaire just because,
and Mother Nature for the poo.

ßP

CATNIP BOOKS
Published by Catnip Publishing Ltd.
320 City Road
London EC1V 2NZ

This edition published 2018
1 3 5 7 9 8 6 4 2

Text copyright © Bianca Pitzorno 2018
Translation © Laura Watkinson 2018
Illustrations copyright © Quentin Blake 2018
Cover Colour © Artful Doodlers
Designed by Ali Ardington

ISBN 978-1-91061-118-0

www.catnippublishing.co.uk

Printed by CPI

Lavinia and the Magic Ring

BIANCA PITZORNO

Illustrated by Quentin Blake

Translation by Laura Watkinson

Note from the Author

The story of Lavinia and the magic ring was born one Christmas Eve at a dinner with my friend Valentina, along with some other people whom there's no need to name, as they were not directly involved in the 'poo' phenomenon.

For some years, Valentina had been in the habit of asking me for stories about poo and pee, and I would always oblige. In total, I must have come up with about fifty such stories for her.

That evening, after I'd told her the tale of Lavinia, Valentina gave me a satisfied smile and said, 'Well done! That was such a great story. Better than all the rest.'

So, as Valentina was about to finish her first year at primary school and was already very good at reading, I decided to transform the story of the magic ring from the oral tradition into writing and to make it into a book for her and for other young story lovers.

WARNING!

Reading this book is not recommended for people who are too squeamish.

CONTENTS

The Little Match Girl

It was Christmas Eve in Milan.

All that afternoon, Piazza del Duomo and the streets and shops in the city centre had been packed with huge crowds of people pushing and shoving as they finished their Christmas shopping. The people of Milan rushed by, loaded up with parcels and packages. They were in a hurry to get home, because early that afternoon it had started to get terribly cold.

Then, at around five o'clock, it began to snow. Before long, the statue of Vittorio Emanuele in the centre of the piazza was covered in snow.

'Just as well it's already dark and the pigeons have gone to bed. Otherwise their little legs would freeze,' Lavinia remarked. 'But I wonder where the pigeons go to sleep . . . Maybe up there on the roof of the cathedral? But aren't they frightened, surrounded by all those statues of monsters and saints?'

By now, the spires of the cathedral had all become white as well, as if they were made of candyfloss.

People went dashing past and no one noticed a little match girl, blue with cold, sitting on a step in a ragged dress and offering her boxes of matches to the passers-by.

Every now and then someone stumbled over her bare feet. They would stagger, try to keep their balance, mutter a couple of swear words, like 'Drat it!' or 'Blast!' or even worse, and then, finally, they would see the little girl.

Instead of buying her matches though, the people just hurled insults at her: 'Go home, you scruffy little urchin!', 'Ugh, do you really think that's a suitable place for you to be sitting? Look at you in your filthy rags!' and 'Go on, scram! If I were your father, I'd give you a good hiding!'

And when the girl timidly said, in a hoarse little croak that was interrupted by violent coughing fits, 'Lovely matches, sir! Will you buy my matches?' the irritated passers-by replied: 'Shove your matches, you little pest! What do you expect me to do with matches? Do you think I'm so poor that I don't have a lighter?' Others would shriek indignantly: 'I don't smoke, you filthy brat! I've just given it up and now you're trying to make me start again! You should be ashamed of yourself, you pesky little ragamuffin!'

And they headed home, furiously thinking: *It's Christmas Eve! Why did I have to see that little killjoy tonight of all nights? Meeting a starving, shivering match girl on Christmas Eve? That's got to be bad luck. Now I'm going to feel guilty for the rest of the year!*

Lavinia, because she was indeed that little match girl, really didn't mean to make any of them feel guilty. All she wanted was to sell matches to earn a little money so that she could buy herself a hot chocolate with cream and some biscuits, because she hadn't eaten for three days. And maybe even a pair of fur-lined shoes, because her feet were covered in scabs and chilblains, and they were really sore.

But no one, absolutely no one at all, bought even a single box of matches from her.

At around eight o'clock, a policeman approached her, wrapped up snugly in his blue uniform. He was in a bad mood because he had to work that night instead of being at home with his children, preparing the Christmas crib nativity scene. Prodding her from a distance, with his foot – a little cautiously, because Lavinia really was very filthy indeed – he said to her: 'Oi, you can't sell matches without a licence. In fact, you can't sell anything without a licence. I really ought to arrest you but it's Christmas, so I'll turn a blind eye this time. But you need to make yourself scarce! Now! Got it? Go on – scram! Go home!'

That was easy enough for him to say! Lavinia didn't have a home to go to. She was a little match girl, and little match girls don't have homes.

So it was the policeman who left instead, blowing on his fingers to warm them up, while the little girl remained on the steps of the chemist's shop, numb with cold, starving and with empty pockets, as the last of the Christmas shoppers left the piazza and headed for their tram stops.

The Christmas tree in the middle of the square shone with a thousand lights. But Lavinia knew that if she went closer, they wouldn't warm her, because they weren't real candle flames, just low-voltage lightbulbs.

Besides, in order to get closer to the tree, she

would have had to leave her shelter and go out into the snow, which was still floating down prettily, like a scene on a Christmas card.

Lavinia was only seven years old, but she was an expert in such matters, because as long as she could remember she had always been a little homeless match girl, and she'd had to learn for herself where to find the most comfortable shelters and how to stay as warm as she could.

Night fell. The piazza was deserted now. Only the lights of the advertisements moved, creating an illusion of life and warmth, but the night was just getting colder and colder.

Pulling her rags more tightly around herself, Lavinia curled up in the corner, leaned her head against the wall and fell asleep.

The Fairy Makes Her Appearance

While Lavinia slept, in houses throughout the city, children were watching their mothers and fathers serving up another helping of dinner, and protesting: 'Noooo, I don't want any more! I'm so full! If you make me eat even one more little bite, I'm going to be sick!'

Their parents were shocked. 'This is disgraceful behaviour! Fancy being so fussy about your food – and on Christmas Eve too! Think about all those poor little starving children in Africa. I'm sure they'd love to have your dinner.'

Lavinia wasn't in Africa, but even in her sleep she still felt hungry. She would have given anything for just one little bite of food. If only those parents who were so good at lecturing their children had bought a few boxes of matches before going home and sitting down for dinner!

She was dreaming about roast turkey and huge cakes, mountains of chips, lasagne, meatballs, salami and ice cream and about potato salad – and about the cannelloni with ricotta and spinach that she'd seen in the window of a nearby delicatessen, but there was no way she'd ever be able to afford to taste it.

Towards midnight, Lavinia's dreams were interrupted by the screech of brakes. The little girl looked up and saw a beautiful lady stepping out of a taxi in front of her. She wasn't dressed very suitably for such a cold night. She had a low-cut dress made of a very transparent blue material (so transparent, in fact, that Lavinia

could see her knickers – they were blue too),
bare ankles, velvet slippers, and on her head –
Lavinia had to put her hand over her mouth
to stop herself from laughing – the woman
was wearing the strangest hat imaginable. It
was a kind of long upside-down funnel, and it
sparkled like a Christmas tree.

There are some crazy people in the world!
thought Lavinia, but she went on enjoying the
spectacle, as she was wide awake now.

The lady paid the taxi driver, who gave her
five deep bows, one after another: it must have
been a very good tip. Then she headed towards
Lavinia.

Ooh! thought the little girl. *Maybe the mad
lady's going to buy all of my matches!*

However, when she reached Lavinia, the lady
just bent forward, held out a cigarette and said:
'Excuse me, do you have a light?'

Oh, what should I say to her? Lavinia thought.

Shall I tell her, yes, I've got some matches, but she'll have to pay me for them? No, that wouldn't be nice. And besides, she only needs one, not a whole box.

And so, with a very grand and ladylike gesture, Lavinia opened a new box, struck a match and held it out to the woman, who lit the cigarette without bringing it to her mouth and sucking in, but as if it were a candle, before swiftly raising her hand in the air. A bright fountain erupted from the cigarette – a spray of sparks like a firework display!

She really is mad, thought Lavinia. *Doesn't she have anything better to do at this time of night? Doesn't she have a nice warm house to sleep in?*

She's going to catch her death of cold in that flimsy, low-cut dress!

Then she plucked up courage and asked the woman, 'Excuse me, but are you going to a fancy-dress party?'

'No, why do you ask?' the stranger replied.

'Well, why are you dressed like that?'

'Oh, because I'm a fairy, of course!' said the woman, as if it were the most natural thing in the world.

Lavinia thought: *Yep, now I'm sure of it. She really is completely bonkers. Fairies only exist in books.*

As if the woman had read her mind, she looked Lavinia up and down and then said, 'How strange. Normally you only find little match girls in stories.'

They studied each other suspiciously. Neither of them wanted to be made a fool of.

After a pause, the woman said to Lavinia: 'I

am real. Honestly. Try giving me a pinch!' Then, without any warning, she reached out one hand and pinched Lavinia's arm.

'Ow!' shrieked the little girl. 'It was me who was supposed to be pinching you!' So she gave the woman a kick, but it didn't really hurt her because Lavinia's feet were bare.

'Now we're even,' the fairy said calmly. 'And now we're both certain that the other one exists. Lavinia, you have been most kind and generous to me. I would like to repay you for giving me one of your matches for free.'

Great! Now she's going to give me loads of money! the little girl thought excitedly. *She's going to transport me to the palace of a prince who'll marry me! She'll make me absolutely beautiful! But what good will that do me? Oh, I know, people will pay to see me and I'll be able to use the money to buy tons of things to eat.*

'I would like to give you a most exceptional

gift,' continued the fairy. 'A magic ring. Ta-da!'

She took a ring from a pocket in her see-through dress and slipped it onto Lavinia's finger. It was just a plain little ring, without any decoration or jewels.

'What does it do?' asked Lavinia, hoping that its simple appearance concealed some fabulous power.

The fairy just started laughing to herself, like the madwoman she was.

'What does it do?' Lavinia insisted.

'What does it do? It turns things into poo.'

'Whaaaat?!'

'It turns things into poo. Have you gone deaf?' asked the fairy with an angelic smile.

The Magic of the Ring

Lavinia started whining. 'Well, what a great present! Seriously, this ring is the last thing I need! I'm already so unlucky – with no home, no mother, freezing to death and with an empty stomach . . . and then you come along and give me a gift like this!' And she tried to pull the ring off her finger – but it wouldn't budge.

'It's yours for ever now,' said the fairy. 'You'll never be able to lose it. But it's not as useless as you seem to think. Quite the opposite! If you use your intelligence, you'll see that you can do great things with the power of this ring. You just have to be smart about it.'

Lavinia went on turning the ring on her finger and watched, open-mouthed, as the advertisement hoarding in front of her suddenly turned brown, collapsing in on itself and becoming a soft and stinky heap on the pavement.

'You see?' said the fairy. 'You've worked out what to do all by yourself. But the instructions are as follows: if you want to transform something into poo, you need to stare at it as you turn the ring around your finger in a clockwise direction. If you want it to return to its original state, you have to stare and turn the ring in the opposite direction. And please be careful. You don't want to make any mistakes.'

With a whistle, she summoned a passing taxi, leaped into it and disappeared.

Feeling rather stunned, the little match girl thought to herself: *Was it all just a dream?*

But the ring was on her finger, and the heap of poo was still steaming away in the cold of the night.

So, to see if the instructions really worked, she stared at the poo, and held her nose, as she turned the ring the other way. The advertisement promptly stood back up again, as clean and shiny as it had been before.

'Good,' said Lavinia. 'At least the instructions work. Hmm . . . but now I have to think of the best way to use this weird magic.'

A Strange Customer

It was Christmas Eve in Milan.

Mr Massimiliano Marsupiali, the owner of an elegant shoe shop, had not yet returned home, where his wife, Cunegonda, and their two children were waiting to start their special Christmas Eve dinner. As usual, Mr Marsupiali had stayed behind after work to count the money he'd made that day.

It was a whole heap of money, because the shop was right in the centre of Milan and, over the course of the morning and the afternoon, up until closing time, thousands of people had come in to buy shoes, boots and slippers. It had seemed as if all the people of Milan had suddenly found themselves barefoot and felt an urgent need to cover their feet. As a result, the shelves were almost empty now, and Mr Massimiliano Marsupiali's cash register was bulging with banknotes.

His assistants had tidied up and gone home, and now Massimiliano was enjoying the warmth of the deserted shop, as he arranged his banknotes into stacks and daydreamed about what he might buy for himself after depositing most of them in the bank.

Mr Massimiliano Marsupiali was so completely absorbed in his Christmas dreams that he didn't even notice the girl with her nose pressed up against the glass of his display window who was trying to catch his attention.

Finally though, the *tap-tap-tap* got through to him and made him look up. And immediately a red flush of rage rushed from his fat neck to his fat face. *Whaaat? At this time? Another of those dratted beggars?* Furiously, he hurried to the door, opened it wide and yelled at the girl, 'Clear off, you scrounger! Get your filthy paws off my window!'

The girl moved her hands and put them behind her back, hiding them from his sight. She started walking towards the door of the shop. Her bare, frozen feet brushed across the layer of snow that covered the pavement. She looked about seven years old, with scruffy hair that might have been blonde under all the dirt, and an angelic face covered in black smudges where she'd wiped away her tears.

As she calmly looked at him, Mr Massimiliano Marsupiali stood at the door as if to block her way.

'What do you want?' he growled.

'A pair of fur-lined boots. Those ones over there, please. I hope you have them in my size!' said the little girl, pointing at a pair of sky-blue boots on a shelf.

'And what about the money? Do you have any money to pay for them?' Mr Marsupiali barked. 'Anyway, the shop's closed. Clear off!'

'Please!' the little girl gently insisted. 'Didn't you see my bare feet? I'm freezing and I'm going to catch a cold. And it's Christmas Eve too. Please be kind and give me those boots.'

'You cheeky little brat! Do you know how much those boots cost?'

'No,' Lavinia confessed. 'And I don't care. Because I don't have any money to pay for them anyway. I want you to give them to me as a present.'

'Ah, really?! A present? And why on earth should I do that?'

'Because I have bare feet and it's cold,'

repeated the girl, gazing around the shelves at the shoes that were left. There weren't that many of them, in fact. It looked as if the shop had been looted.

'Out!' yelled Mr Massimiliano Marsupiali. 'Clear off, you little ragamuffin!' and he turned to close the door.

But he froze when he saw on his shelves, instead of shoes and slippers, lots and lots of little piles of poo.

Outside, in the piazza, the girl was walking away with tiny footsteps, carefully placing her bare feet on the snow.

'Come back here at once, you little wretch!

What did you just do?' Mr Marsupiali yelled from the doorway, his shouts echoing across the deserted square.

Lavinia turned around and smiled. 'You've changed your mind? Fantastic! After all, it *is* Christmas Eve.' And she started walking back to the shop.

'Changed my mind?! I'm calling the police. I'm going to have you arrested, you beggar! Look at the mess you've made!'

'Me?' said the little girl with surprise, 'but I didn't even go into the shop!'

Mr Massimiliano Marsupiali scratched his head. Clearly something wasn't right . . . But as he stood there wondering, he smelled the stink of poo behind him, which was becoming stronger and stronger.

He turned around. The drawer of the cash register, which he'd left half-open while he was counting the cash, was now filled with the same substance as the shelves: stinking, steaming poo. It was so full, in fact, that quite a lot of the poo had overflowed onto the floor.

'My earnings for an entire day . . .' he whispered, his face turning pale. *Maybe this is all just a bad dream*, he thought. But that smell! It was getting worse and worse.

The little girl smiled at him from the shop doorway, taking care not to put her dirty feet on the immaculate carpet.

'Can you do something about this, you little witch?' asked Mr Marsupiali.

Clasping her hands behind her back, the little girl smiled and stared at the shelves. 'I would like those boots,' she said. 'The sky-blue ones, please.' And she told him her size.

Mr Marsupiali turned to see that all the shoes had reappeared on the shelves.

Just as he was about to yell, 'Right. Now I'm going to throw you out!', he turned to look at the cash register. It still had a big pile of poo inside it where his money should have been.

'When I get the boots,' the little girl said sweetly, reading his mind.

Ten minutes later, Lavinia, sitting at the bottom of the statue of Vittorio Emanuele, was lacing up her new boots. Through her tattered dress, she could feel the cold, wet snow.

'Now I need to find myself some new clothes,' she said to herself, standing up and heading for the elegant Galleria, the nearby shopping arcade.

The Night Porter

It was three o'clock on Christmas morning in Milan.

The night porter at the city's most stylish hotel, the Grand Hotel Excelsior Super Deluxe, was snoozing and keeping a lazy eye on the shiny Rolls Royce that was parked outside the entrance for the use of the guests.

The hotel lobby had been quite busy up until about half an hour before, when the last night owls had returned from their evenings out. Now though, everything was deserted and silent.

Outside on the street, the snow was falling, and a soft white layer had already collected on the roof of the Rolls Royce.

Stepping lightly on the carpet of white, a little girl came walking towards the night porter. The man, whose name was Giuseppe Pappalardo, rubbed his eyes and noticed that the girl's feet left hardly any trace on the snow.

What a strange child, he thought to himself. She was wearing the most beautiful pair of sky-blue boots and a fur coat with the hood pulled down over an elegant woollen hat. From beneath the fur emerged a pair of knickerbockers made of the finest Shetland wool – the night porter was able to recognise such luxurious clothes at a glance – and a colourful scarf was wrapped two or three times around her neck, in the latest fashion.

She was a little rich girl – there was no doubt about it. But why hadn't she washed her face

before coming out? And what about her hair? Her long, curly hair was so incredibly tangled and dirty that you couldn't even tell what colour it was.

The girl approached the glass door of the hotel. She placed one hand on the knob, and Giuseppe Pappalardo saw that they were even dirtier than her face, with black around her nails and her fingers red and cracked with chilblains.

Aww, she must be one of those little girls who's always losing her gloves, thought the night porter. *Maybe she's been in a car accident. Maybe she's lost her parents or her nanny. She probably just wants to use the telephone.*

It didn't even occur to him to chase her away and call her a beggar or a ragamuffin, because the clothes that the little girl was wearing were not rags, and anyone who can afford such expensive garments can also allow themselves the luxury of not washing very often.

'Rich people – they're so eccentric!' the night porter muttered with a sigh. 'Fancy letting your child go out in that state!'

He walked towards the girl. 'Would you like to phone home?' he asked politely. 'Or should I contact the police for you?'

'No, thanks,' she replied. 'I want a room. The best room in the hotel.'

Lavinia Makes Herself at Home

The night porter peered out into the snow, looking down to the end of the street, to the left and the right, to see if the little girl's parents might be coming. But the street was deserted.

'What are you looking for? There's no one out there. I'm all alone,' said Lavinia.

Yes, it was indeed Lavinia, dressed in a completely new outfit, which she'd acquired using a similar method as with the boots.

'Well, we can't offer accommodation to unaccompanied children,' said the porter. 'But maybe I can make an exception this time. Yes, I'll do it for you. After all, it *is* Christmas.'

'Thank you. And, by the way, happy Christmas!' Lavinia said sweetly.

'And the same to you. Um, do you know how much a room in this hotel costs? I'm sure you must. You've probably been here lots of times with your . . .'

'Nope. No idea,' replied Lavinia. 'I've never set foot here before this evening. And I don't care how much a room costs. Because I don't have any money to pay for it anyway.'

'We can't accept cheques from children. But maybe in this case I could make another exception,' said the night porter. 'Would you please be so kind as to show me some form of ID?'

'Some . . . form . . . of what?'

'An identity card, a passport . . . Something with your name written on it.'

Lavinia unbuttoned her fur coat and unzipped her knickerbockers, and the night porter looked on in amazement as she started rummaging around in her underwear, where she usually kept a small notebook and a pencil.

Before this miraculous night, her knickers had been her only item of clothing without rips and holes in, so she used them as a safe place to keep her treasures.

Concentrating very hard, Lavinia scratched out a few letters with the pencil on a piece of paper from the notebook, tore it out and handed it to the night porter.

'What's this supposed to be?' asked Giuseppe Pappalardo.

'Don't you know how to read?' replied the little girl. 'It's something with my name written on it.'

And indeed, on the grubby and crumpled piece of paper, was written the word,

LAVINIA.

'But that won't do, sweetheart!' the man said with a smile. 'It has to be an official document.' Meanwhile he was thinking to himself: *Children! They're such scamps!* He had seven children of his own at home, and his eldest son, in particular, was his pride and joy.

'Now listen,' Lavinia said impatiently. 'I got the boots without paying for them. They just gave me the clothes without asking for any kind of documents. So why are you making such a fuss?'

The man looked at her suspiciously. *Without paying? Is she a thief? Well, that changes things. It changes them a lot.*

'So those clothes don't actually belong to you?' he said.

'They do now,' replied Lavinia.

'But what about before that?'

'Huh, that's nice! What do you think? Before that, they belonged to the shopkeeper. It's not like I was born wearing clothes. What about your clothes? Didn't you get them from a shop?'

'Yes, but I paid for them!'

'And I didn't. They gave them to me – and that's that!'

'As a present, you mean?'

'Yes, let's just say they gave them to me as a present . . . in exchange for a little favour.'

'Right, I think you're starting to waste my time. I don't need any favours, and I can't give you a room for free.'

'Are you sure about that?' said Lavinia. She looked up and stared at the two big crystal chandeliers that were hanging in the middle of the lobby. As she did so, she clasped her hands behind her back . . .

The night porter followed her gaze and then grabbed the edge of his desk, thinking, *Maybe I drank too much wine at home this evening before my shift.*

The chandeliers seemed to be trembling and changing colour! He watched as they turned soft and brown and trickled off the chains they were hanging from, dropping like ripe pieces of fruit and – sploosh! – plopping down onto the beautiful Persian carpet.

At the same moment, an unmistakable stink of fresh poo filled the entire lobby.

'You see? Now you need a favour too,' said Lavinia, stepping back towards the lifts and wrinkling her nose at the smell.

'B– but,' stuttered poor, astonished Giuseppe. 'What on earth just happened? Oh dear, oh dear, oh dear! How am I ever going to clean this up before the manager gets here?'

'Be careful not to step in it,' Lavinia warned

him as he hurried from behind the desk to go
and fetch a bucket of water and a mop.

She waited until he'd gone and then turned
the ring the other way.

When Giuseppe returned, puffing and
panting, the two chandeliers were back,
glittering away as they hung from the stuccoed
ceiling.

'You see?' the little girl said to the night porter,
who was standing there as if struck by lightning.
'You needed a favour, and I did you one. So now
will you give me the key to the best room in the
hotel?'

'Yes, yes, I'll give you the key, but you'll have
to talk to the manager tomorrow, and I don't
think he'll let you get away with it that easily.'

A New Life for Lavinia

That night Lavinia slept in a warm, soft bed between lovely clean sheets. She was so tired that it didn't even occur to her to have a bath before tucking herself in (after all, it *was* past three o'clock in the morning) and so she made both the pillowcase and the sheets thoroughly filthy, particularly around her feet.

The next day, she got up early so that she could explore her room. She had a huge TV, a telephone and her own little drinks bar. One door led into the bathroom, which was full of shiny marble and golden taps. Another door opened into a living room, with antique furniture and fresh flowers in vases on the mantelpiece and the breakfast table.

Lavinia walked into the bathroom. She washed her hair and had a nice shower and thought: *Today's a holiday. And tomorrow too. But as soon as the shops open up again, I'll have to get myself some new undies.*

It was true. Her old knickers, even though they didn't have any holes in, and her tattered old vest didn't go with the elegant clothes she'd been given the night before. She didn't have any socks at all, tatty or otherwise. But then, has anyone ever seen a little match girl wearing socks? Luckily though, she'd chosen long boots, so no one would notice her lack of socks.

When she was dressed, she had a moment of uncertainty. She wasn't quite sure whether to ring the bell to order breakfast in the room, or to go downstairs and eat in the hotel restaurant. In the end, she decided to go down, as she was a friendly girl and she wanted to meet the other guests.

Lavinia chose a table in the middle of the room so that she had a good view of everything. Then she ordered a very big breakfast: hot chocolate with cream, fresh bread, butter, five kinds of jam, freshly baked honey scones, ham and eggs, grapefruit juice, waffles, croissants, oatmeal and raisins, puffed rice and a selection of cheeses.

Maybe that sounds like too much for breakfast. But don't forget that Lavinia hadn't eaten anything for three days, and she hadn't had a full stomach for years. The night before, when she'd been so thrilled about the powers of the magic ring, she'd only thought about getting a complete new outfit, and she'd forgotten her hunger in all the excitement.

After a good night's sleep though, her hunger had come back, even more strongly than before, so it made sense that the little match girl couldn't resist the temptation when she saw all the wonderful food that was on offer.

The poor little thing had never had a proper upbringing, so she threw herself upon the breakfast, stuffing her face and spilling food all over her new clothes.

As she did so, the manager of the hotel entered the restaurant, dressed in black like a penguin. The day porter had told him the strangest story, which the night porter had told the day porter when they changed shifts. But it was a rather confused tale. All the manager had grasped was that some girl or other had taken up residence in the hotel's best suite, and that she was unable to pay the bill.

He asked a waiter to point out Lavinia to him, and then he marched up to her and barked, 'Is it true you don't have any money?'

'Yep. Happy Christmas, sir,' Lavinia replied politely, her knife poised in mid-air.

'Then you will have to leave!' the manager snarled, ignoring her Christmas wishes.

'Really?' asked Lavinia, who was getting used to this by now.

'I'm calling the police,' said the manager, 'and having you arrested. You owe me for a night's accommodation and breakfast. And if you can't pay, then you're going to prison. So pay up!'

'But I already told you I've got no money!' replied the little girl.

'Then you must stop eating, right this instant! Do you have any idea how much all this food costs? Such a cheek! Spit out that cheese! It's not yours. You can't afford it!'

Lavinia noisily spat the cheese onto the floor, and then she started bawling, not because she was really upset, but because embarrassing the manager was so much fun.

An Eventful Breakfast

When Lavinia started crying, people from all the other tables turned round to stare; they looked curious, annoyed and shocked. They were the kind of people who were used to silent and sophisticated surroundings and who really couldn't stand anyone making a fuss.

The furious manager grabbed the girl by the collar and lifted her up out of her chair. But Lavinia grabbed on to the tablecloth, tipping her fried eggs onto him, and all of the other food ended up on the floor.

'Look at the
mess you've made!'
the manager hissed.

'Oops! Hang on!' said
Lavinia, clasping her hands and
staring at the chaos she had created.
On the pale grey carpet, where the broken
plates and spilled food had been only a moment
before, a big, nasty stain appeared, as if someone
had walked in poo, spreading it all around.

'What on earth?!' squawked the manager.

'This is outrageous!' the elegant hotel guests
exclaimed at the nearby tables, grabbing their

napkins and burying
their noses in them.

Lavinia though, was still
not satisfied. She saw a waiter
walking by with a tray of food up on his
head. Turning the ring, she stared at the food.
Suddenly the tray was full of poo – and the
waiter didn't even notice. He then placed it,
with an elegant sweep, on the table where a very
wealthy lady was sitting with an admirer.

The poo stank and steamed away on the plate. The lady shrieked and then fainted, and her friend only just managed to stop her ending up head first in the tray of poo.

The people at the other tables watched in horror. But Lavinia was using the power of her gaze like a whip now, lashing one table and the next, with poo appearing in all shapes and sizes on every plate where the food had been.

The furious guests rose to their feet and pushed back their chairs.

'That's quite enough!' they cried. 'This is outrageous! We're going to call the police! We'll report you to the Institute of Hygiene! We will never set foot in this filthy restaurant again!'

The manager was weeping in despair by now. Lavinia played it cool and dried her nose and her tears on a corner of the tablecloth.

'I'm ruined,' groaned the manager, collapsing onto the chair in front of her.

'So can I stay in my suite?' said Lavinia. 'If you let me stay, I'll make everything go back to the way it was. Look!'

And with one glance all around, and a swift turn of the ring, she instantly turned the plates and the tablecloths, the trays and the carpets back to normal – even the stench disappeared!

Everyone was so stunned that they froze like statues. Everyone except for the manager. He grabbed Lavinia's arm. 'Stay? I don't think so! I'm going to throw you out, right this instant, you filthy little witch! And I'm going to fire that idiot Pappalardo for allowing you to enter the premises.'

Then he took her by the neck and dragged her into the lobby. But Lavinia managed to free her hands and, twisting the ring, she looked up. One of the enormous chandeliers transformed into a mountain of poo and dropped down right on top of the manager, completely covering him.

'And I'm not going to turn that back again,' said Lavinia, who had dodged it at the last second. 'You'll have to get rid of it yourself. I expect the smell will hang around for quite a while. Now listen carefully, because if you don't, I'll turn the entire hotel into poo. Pappalardo gets to keep his job and I'm going back to my suite. Where no one will disturb me. Got it?'

And that was how Lavinia's new life began.

She had a comfortable place to sleep and an entire wardrobe of new clothes, and she could eat as much as she wanted. A thousand times, she whispered her secret thanks to the fairy who had given her the magic ring, and she always made sure she used her gift carefully.

Now that she was no longer hungry or cold and she didn't have to beg or try to sell matches that no one wanted, she learned not to judge things by their appearance too.

After all, who would have thought that something like poo, which everyone hates so much, could turn out to be so very, very precious?

Lavinia Finds a Friend

Of course, if you have a brain in your head, you'll have realised that Lavinia's story can't end there.

The ring that the fairy had given her that freezing Christmas Eve finally allowed her to satisfy her most important needs, like clothes to wear, food to eat, and a warm bed to sleep in. However, it could also make less sensible wishes come true, and that often results in problems, or at least it does in storybooks.

Lavinia lived happily at the Grand Hotel

Excelsior Super Deluxe, where she was respected by everyone and pampered by Giuseppe Pappalardo, who was grateful for how she'd defended him and stopped the manager from firing him. Even the manager was really nice to her now. Some people are funny like that.

Lavinia liked to make good use of her time. Every morning she booked the Rolls Royce and visited the zoo to chat with the animals. They taught her a lot of interesting things about the countries they came from, but the main thing she learned was that all of the animals – locked away inside their cages, being stared at and teased by visitors – were very unhappy.

They had everything that little match girls

usually don't: a nice, warm home and food
to eat every day. But that didn't matter. They
would much rather have been cold and hungry,
but free. Lavinia believed that everyone should
have what they preferred, no matter what others
might think, and so she decided to use her magic
to free her animal friends.

It was not going to be easy though. The plan
needed a lot of careful thought and perhaps
some discussion with someone who knew more
than she did.

Once again, Lavinia realised that she was
missing something very important: a friend.
And a friend was something that the magic ring
couldn't get for her.

If you turn someone into poo, or threaten to
turn everything they care about into poo, maybe
they'll do as you say and be afraid of you, but
they certainly won't like you. Lavinia was very
well aware of that.

In February though, Giuseppe Pappalardo's oldest son came to work at the hotel, as a liftboy. His name was Peppino and he was a funny-looking boy, as thin as a rake, with sticking-out teeth and wingnut ears. He was so very, very clever that he'd finished primary school at the age of seven, and high school when he was eleven. But now that his compulsory education was over, he had to go out to work to help the family.

'Everyone said to me: "Well done! You're so lucky to be so clever!" Ha! While other boys of my age are going to school and spending the rest of their time playing, I'm so intelligent that – lucky me! – I get to spend eight and a half hours a day making a lift go up and down, and the police won't come to complain to my father or to the manager, because I've already completed my compulsory education.'

Lavinia didn't really understand difficult words like 'compulsory education', but she could see how much the boy was missing school. She'd never been to school, and she would have loved to go. But who ever heard of a little match girl going to school?

The few letters she knew how to write – her name for example – she had painstakingly learned from advertising posters or from watching television in shop windows. But she really hated being so uneducated.

So when Peppino arrived, she seized the opportunity. She started spending most of her time in the lift, going up and down from the ground floor to the tenth floor with him.

Whenever there were no other guests in the lift, Peppino taught her fascinating things like times tables, grammar, the tributaries of the River Po, and the poetry of Giovanni Pascoli.

And, as they went up and down, Lavinia learned lots and lots of interesting things.

An Expedition to the Zoo

'So,' Lavinia said to Peppino one day, 'when are we going to free the animals from the zoo?'

'As soon as I have an afternoon off,' he replied.

'And when will that be?'

'Let me take a look at my diary. Ermmm . . . Yep, on Thursday.'

So, on Thursday afternoon, Lavinia and Peppino walked together to the zoo, which wasn't far from the Grand Hotel Excelsior Super Deluxe. As they walked, they discussed their plan.

'I could turn the bars of the cages into poo, and the zookeepers too,' Lavinia suggested.

'Great idea! So the animals, including the really scary ones, will start wandering around the city, causing who knows what kind of trouble. The carnivorous ones might even start eating people!'

'Not me. They won't eat me, because I'm their friend.'

'Yes, but that won't stop them gobbling up other people. And in a city like ours the herbivores would die of starvation. Does that sound like a sensible plan?'

'What do you suggest then?'

'Funny you should ask. Here's my idea: the two of us need to hide at the zoo and wait until it gets dark. And then we can call the animals out of their sleeping areas and you can turn them into poo.'

'But I want to free them! Not turn them into

poo!' protested Lavinia.

'Hang on. I've not finished. We'll hide in the bushes and wait until morning. When the zookeepers arrive, they'll think the animals are still asleep inside their dens, and they'll clean out the enclosures with those long-handled shovels that they stick through the bars. I've been asking around, and they always collect all the poo and send it to a fertiliser company in the back of a lorry. Before the lorry leaves though, we'll, steal it and put it on a ship to Africa . . . But you'll need to turn the poo back into animals first so that when they arrive they'll be able to make their way straight to the jungle.'

'But how am I going to turn them back again if they're locked up inside the lorry?' Lavinia wailed. 'You know I have to stare at them while I twist the ring. Otherwise the magic doesn't work.'

'I've thought about
that too. Look, I've
brought along a drill.
We can use it to make holes in the back of the
lorry so that the animals will be able to breathe
on their journey. I'll make one of the holes a bit
bigger so that you can look inside and undo the
magic.'

'That sounds good,' said Lavinia. 'You really
have thought of everything. You're so clever,
Peppino!'

t the animals began their long journey to Africa, and the two satisfied friends made their way back to the Grand Hotel Excelsior Super Deluxe, where Peppino had to start his next shift on the elevators.

Lavinia the Hero

As Lavinia and Peppino were crossing Piazza Cavour, they heard a lot of commotion – screams, sirens wailing, deafening whistles and another, louder noise, a scary, hissing, rumbling sound that was growing louder and louder.

They looked towards the noise and saw a massive fire devouring a five-storey building. Huge flames and thick columns of black smoke were rising from the windows.

'Oh, look! It's so beautiful!' said Lavinia, stopping to watch the unusual spectacle. (Little match girls have always enjoyed playing with fire, even though it's a dangerous game.)

'You idiot!' Peppino yelled at her, taking her arm and dragging her towards the people who were trying to put out the fire.

The firefighters were there with their red fire engines, their ladders and their hoses. The ambulances were there too, and the police, who were trying to keep away nosy onlookers. But even with the powerful jets of water coming from the hoses, the flames continued to rise higher and higher, eating up the shutters on the windows and making the walls and ceilings collapse.

'Is there anyone still inside?' asked Peppino in a worried voice.

'No. Luckily the residents all managed to get out in time,' someone replied. But then, as if to prove him wrong, they heard the cries of a small child coming from a window on the ground floor.

A young woman who was standing in the crowd with a group of toddlers let out a scream and fainted into the arms of a fireman. It turned out that she ran the nursery school that was on the ground floor of the burning building. When the alarm had sounded, she had gathered together all the children in the playroom and helped them out through the window, passing them, one by one, into the hands of the firefighters. The children had thought it was great fun, and there was no way any of them wanted to go home now. They all meant to stay and enjoy the show until the end.

The nursery teacher had counted them, and she'd thought they were all there.

She'd completely forgotten about the littlest one though, who had been put in the crib for a nap. Alessandro Testarossa was only one year old, and he'd been at the nursery school for just a few days. The teacher still hadn't got used to including him in the number of her little charges. As she didn't see him with the others when they made their escape, she'd left him behind in the panic.

Now the noise and the heat had woken little Alessandro and he was shrieking away like an angry eagle.

His mother, who worked at the bakery across the road, had come running, and now she was screaming: 'Do something, please! Somebody save my baby!'

But the flames were so high now that no one could enter the building. All that the firefighters could do was aim their jets of water into the window, flooding the room and giving little Alessandro a shower. Wet through and terrified, he carried on wailing even more loudly. The flames faltered briefly before coming back, even higher than before and surrounding the crib in a circle that was closing in on him.

Lavinia was watching the scene with her mouth wide open, fascinated and paralysed with fear, when she felt a nudge in her back. It was Peppino, and he pushed her right through the police barriers, all the way to the window. 'Do something – now!' he ordered her, lifting her up so that she could see into the room. 'Put out the fire!'

'What do you expect me to do if even the firefighters can't handle it?' whimpered Lavinia.

'Use the ring, stupid!'

So Lavinia stared at the flames, which were now touching the crib, and twisted the ring around her finger. As the stunned crowd watched, the flames disappeared and little Alessandro found himself surrounded by a sea of poo.

As she was already there, Lavinia also looked at the windows on the higher floors and immediately the flames trickled onto the windowsills and down the building, changing colour and consistency. Inside, where Lavinia's stare did not reach, the fire was still crackling away, but the worst of the danger was over.

Little Alessandro hadn't realised he'd been rescued yet, so he went on sobbing.

His mum, two firefighters, a policewoman and a paramedic all rushed over to the window at the same time, and so did the nursery teacher, who had come round after someone gave her cheeks a slap.

When they got to the window though, they all stopped in their tracks and started being super polite to one another.

'No, no, please. I insist. You go first,' the policewoman said to Alessandro's mother. 'We don't want to spoil the moment. You should be the one to give your baby his first hug!'

'Oh dear, oh dear,' replied Mrs Testarossa. 'I don't want to upset the firefighters. They're the ones who are supposed to carry people to safety, aren't they?'

'But the danger's over now,' said the firefighters. 'The little boy might be injured. It's probably best if a paramedic takes care of him.'

'Waaahhh! Waaaaah!' screamed poor little poo-covered Alessandro, reaching out his tiny hands towards his reluctant rescuers. 'Waaahhh!'

'Oh, for goodness sake!' yelled the police officer who was in charge. 'Make your minds up! Someone has to get in there and make him stop crying. That baby's going to burst our eardrums!'

'Well, why don't you go?' said the nursery teacher.

'Uhwaaah! Uuuuhwaaaaah!' screamed little Alessandro.

With a sigh, Lavinia grabbed a hose from a firewoman's hand and aimed it at the baby. *Those grown-ups!* she thought to herself. *What a fussy bunch!*

The jet of water hit the crib and little Alessandro got a second soaking.

'Aaaahhh! Aaaaah!' the dripping-wet baby cried, still stretching his arms out towards the adults. Now that the water had washed away the poo, they could go in and rescue him. Lavinia used the same method to clean the whole front of the building, and the firemen went up on their ladders to put out the last few fires that were burning away inside.

And, of course, Lavinia was declared a hero and the mayor gave her a gold medal for her bravery.

Alessandro's mum told Lavinia how grateful she was and invited her to come to the bakery whenever she wanted. She would never have to pay for anything – not even if she ate all the cakes in the shop.

Lavinia Makes a Terrible Mistake

Unfortunately, her adventure with the fire did nothing to improve Lavinia's personality. Quite the opposite, in fact. The little girl started to feel very proud, as if she deserved all the credit for the rescue and it had nothing to do with the ring or with the fairy who had given it to her.

During their lessons in the lift, Peppino tried – and failed – to make her see reason and be a little more modest.

After a while, Lavinia began to find him boring. She was no longer interested in times tables, French irregular verbs, musical scales or the circumference of circles. Even set theory seemed dull.

One day, when Peppino was trying to impress her with his education, Lavinia suddenly said, 'Huh! Who do you think you are? You do know I rescued a baby from a fire in a five-storey building, don't you?'

Slowly but surely, their friendship cooled off.

For one thing, Lavinia – who knows why? – had got the idea into her head that she was incredibly beautiful. Maybe it was because people stared at her everywhere she went. That was obviously just because they'd heard about her magic and thought she was extraordinary for that reason. Beauty had nothing to do with it; in spite of her lovely clothes, her clean hair and everything else, Lavinia was just the same ordinary little match girl she'd always been.

But, once it takes hold of a person, vanity is

hard to control, and this weak spot was about to land Lavinia in a very sticky situation.

One morning, Lavinia was getting ready to go out for her usual riding lesson. The Rolls Royce was waiting for her outside the hotel, with its engine already running.

Lavinia stopped in front of the mirror to straighten her riding hat. It was one of those ridiculous black caps with a peak that makes you look like a baby goose in mourning. As if that would do anything to improve the looks of a little girl who was really only very average-looking!

But Lavinia, blinded by her vanity, spent a long time in front of the mirror, arranging her curls behind her ears, scratching her nose,

licking her lips to make them more shiny, and pulling all those silly faces that women sometimes do when they're getting ready to go out. And as she looked at herself, she thought, *I'm so beautiful! I really am the most stunning girl in the whole city of Milan!*

At that moment, a voice echoed inside her head, a voice that sounded a lot like Peppino's. And it said: 'Hey you! Don't be such a big-head. You're just an ordinary girl. There must be at least a thousand girls in Milan alone who are prettier than you!'

'Hmph, so that's what that idiot Peppino thinks of me!' muttered Lavinia. 'But I know it's just jealousy. Ha, if he was brave enough to say that to my face, I'd turn him into poo . . . Like this!' And she twisted the ring on her finger.

Don't forget that at the same time she was staring at herself in the mirror – and so the ring's magic turned against her!

In an instant, poor Lavinia felt her legs go soft, then the rest of her body, and – splashhh! – she collapsed on the floor as a greenish pile of poo.

Every little bit of her had turned into poo: her head, her stomach, her feet, her nails, her

hair, her clothes, her shoes. Even that ridiculous riding hat with the peak! Everything except the ring, in fact, which couldn't do magic on itself.

A Sticky Situation

Anyone who entered the room wouldn't have found a single trace of Lavinia, except for a riding crop that she'd thrown onto an armchair. And if they'd seen it, they'd just have thought Lavinia was a scatterbrain who had forgotten to take it when she went out.

However, in spite of her transformation, Lavinia was still able to think. And she was thinking furiously, trying to find a way out of this unpleasant situation. She was thinking so hard that her brain was steaming. As her brain had also turned into poo, it was steaming away too, so it looked as if it wasn't just poo she'd turned into, but very fresh poo indeed!

Lavinia knew that all it would take for her to turn back to normal was one look at herself in the mirror as she turned the ring in the other direction. But that was no easy task! Firstly, because the ring was floating in the middle of a soft and squishy mess. So it was impossible to make it turn the way she wanted.

Even if she'd managed to turn the ring, the pile of poo had spread out across the floor, so there was no way she could look at herself in the mirror above the chest of drawers, which seemed so far away now.

Lavinia was furious. Even though she'd been turned into poo, she hadn't lost her senses. She could look, hear, think – and even smell. And that was the most awful thing about it, because the smell of her new body was really bad, and there was no way she could get away from it. It was such a stink that she thought she might faint. But can poo faint?

One thing she certainly couldn't do was move, as she had no muscles now. Even using all of her willpower, all she could do was make the pile of poo tremble slightly, which was nowhere near enough movement to turn the ring.

So, feeling desperate, she started to cry. But she had to stop right away, because the tears were making the mess on the floor even runnier.

As she lay there, trying hard not to panic and to come up with some sort of solution, the door opened – and a very angry Peppino was standing there.

'Lavinia!' he shouted. 'Why are you always so late? You're getting ruder and ruder. That poor driver's been waiting with his engine running for half an hour now!'

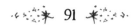

But then he stopped and stood there in the doorway. 'Oh, that's great! Lavinia's not even here! She must have slipped out without me noticing. Perhaps she went through the lobby when I was up in the lift . . . But why didn't she take the Rolls Royce? She must have decided to walk instead and didn't bother to tell the driver. Typical! She's so rude. She doesn't care about anyone else. Huh! I'll go downstairs and let the driver know.'

Meanwhile Lavinia, down there on the floor, was desperately trying to get him to notice her so that she could ask for help. But you couldn't see the chest of drawers from the doorway, so there was no way Peppino would spot her.

Oh, and now he's leaving, Lavinia thought miserably, *and I'm going to be stuck here until the end of time. I'll dry out. Maybe I'll even die . . . What a terrible way to go, turned into a dry poo without anyone knowing that it's me inside.*

*Inside? No, not inside. I AM THE POO! Poor
me! I really have got myself into a mess.*

And even though she knew how dangerous it
was, she started crying again – buckets, this time.

Peppino had decided not to leave yet though,
because he could tell there was something
strange about the room. A smell, an atmosphere
that he couldn't quite pin down, but it was still
making him suspicious . . .

Then he spotted a thin yellowish-green trickle
of poo running out from behind a leather
armchair and towards the door.

He jumped out of the way.

Peppino was a very clean young man and he
polished his leather shoes every day until they
shone like two mirrors. There was no way he
wanted to get poo on them!

'That Lavinia!' he exclaimed. 'That's why she
left without being seen. She's made another of
her messes. But she should just have undone her

magic and turned the ring to clean the room, instead of leaving such a nasty job for the maids. Since she's got so big-headed, she's had no consideration for anyone else. Goodness knows what she turned into poo this time!'

Lavinia tried to communicate with him but she just slid around on the floor, melting in her tears of frustration. *It's me! This time I managed to turn* myself *into poo! Help me, Peppino, and I promise I'll be humble and modest again, like I was when I was just a little match girl.*

Obviously though, Peppino couldn't hear her silent words, and he looked down in disgust at the pile of what had once been his friend Lavinia.

But then the ring came floating along on the river of tears.

He's going to pick it up! thought Lavinia with a sigh of relief. *He'll turn it around to take a look, and maybe the magic will work and transform me back to how I was!*

Peppino didn't recognise the ring though, and he was actually a bit of a squeamish type. 'Ew, look at that piece of metal, all covered in poo!' he said. 'How disgusting! I'd rather die than dirty my hands picking it up!'

All's Well That Ends Well

The situation had come to a standstill. On the one hand, there was Peppino, hesitating in the doorway and trying to decide whether to ignore the mess his friend had made and just leave, or to tidy up the room somehow so that the maids wouldn't be upset.

On the other hand, there was Lavinia, who was dissolving more and more on the floor and moving further away from the mirror, with no way to make Peppino recognise her.

Luckily though, thanks to its magic, the ring

couldn't be detached from her. Otherwise the tears might have carried it away from the poo, and then there really would have been nothing poor Lavinia could do.

Finally Peppino came to a decision. His kindness was stronger than his squeamishness. 'I'm not going to let the maids deal with such a nasty job,' he exclaimed. 'I'll handle this myself!' And he went to look for cleaning equipment.

At that point, Lavinia's tears doubled. She knew that she was in really big trouble now. Peppino was going to wash her away with a bucket and a mop. Or he'd wipe her up and flush her down the loo, and she'd lose the ring or drown – or who knew what else might happen to her?!

When Peppino came back, he noticed that the pile of poo had spread even more and was even runnier now. That was because of all the tears.

How strange, he thought. *Just as well I brought a big bag of sawdust.*

I should explain that, as well as looking after the lifts, Peppino also had to walk the two dogs that belonged to the manager of the Grand Hotel Excelsior Super Deluxe. As he was such a nice, civilised young man, he always took along a little shovel and a bag of special sawdust, which he used to dry and collect the dogs' poos. Now he was intending to use the same method to clean the room.

So he emptied the entire bag of sawdust onto Lavinia, waited for the poo to be absorbed, and then he took the shovel and started scooping the whole mess into a big bin bag.

As he scooped, the shovel moved the ring, turning it the opposite way...

A mirror! A mirror!
Lavinia thought frantically, knowing that if she

couldn't look at herself she wouldn't be able to use the magic. She didn't want to waste this precious opportunity. But – remember? – the poo was on the floor and the mirror was high up on the wall. Poor Lavinia, she was just one step away from being saved, but there was no mirror! It was quite an extreme punishment for her vanity.

Ah, but you hadn't forgotten about Peppino's shiny leather shoes, had you? The ones he polished every morning until they shone like mirrors? Lavinia's desperate gaze fell on the shoes, where she saw, reflected in the shiny black leather, the shovel scooping up the poo.

So she stared as hard as she could at her reflection in the shoe, waiting for the ring to turn again. And the ring turned!

Imagine the fright that Peppino got when Lavinia suddenly appeared at his feet, shaking sawdust off herself!

'You?! Where did you come from?' he cried in
amazement.

'From the poo!' Lavinia replied triumphantly.
'I was the poo this time! Thank goodness you
used sawdust instead of water. And thank
goodness you turned the ring!'

So, as they say, all's well that ends well. The two children aired the room to get rid of the smell. Even though the magic had made every last trace of the poo disappear, they each had a nice shower, giving themselves a good scrub with soap and a flannel.

Then they told the driver that they wanted to go to the cinema and they had a very nice day out.

Lavinia wasn't so snooty and big-headed anymore. She'd been poo herself, even if only for an hour, and the experience had made her wiser. She realised now that she wasn't more important than anyone else and that friendship is so much more valuable than a magic ring.

I haven't heard any news about her latest adventures. But I do know that Lavinia ignored Peppino's advice and didn't get rid of the ring, partly because it was impossible to remove it from her finger. So she still has her amazing magic powers. But clearly she's decided, for now, not to use them and to behave like any other ordinary girl.

If I happen to find out that she's started using the magic ring again though, I promise to come and tell you all about it.

Best Selling Author
BIANCA PITZORNO

In order to inherit his great uncle's millions, Alfonso has to marry a witch. But who believes in witches in the 21st Century and in any case who would want to marry the ghastly Alfonso?

Meanwhile Mr and Mrs Zep's seventh daughter Sybilla is starting to behave rather oddly. She floats in water, cannot see her reflection in a mirror and is the only one who can understand their pet parrot.

So as far as marriage goes will Alfonso know which sister is witch? And which sister can stop his dastardly plan?

Turn over to read the first exciting chapter

The Essential Prologue

A smug little smirk flickered across Alfonso Terribile's lips. Rudely slumped in the lawyer's armchair, he was listening to the reading of his Great-Uncle Sempronio's will, who had passed away the week before from a fatal case of indigestion caused by eating too much fried fish.

Finally, thought Alfonso with satisfaction, *the ancient mummy has popped his clogs!*

Having read just these few lines, my dear readers, you will probably already have worked out that:

a. Great-Uncle Sempronio, when he was alive, had been very rich indeed and, upon his death, he had left a lot of money.
b. Alfonso Terribile was his only heir.
c. Alfonso was a heartless great-nephew who was incredibly selfish and money-grabbing.

What you couldn't have guessed though – but I'll tell you now and you'll have to trust me – is that Alfonso was also a most unattractive young man, with pimples all over his face, a weak chin, and crooked teeth that were turning green because they hadn't been brushed for so long. His greasy hair was full of dandruff, his ears were filthy and there was a black line around the collar of his shirt.

He was also very lazy and had never even contemplated thinking about the idea of work. *After all*, he always said to himself, *sooner or later I'll get my inheritance from Great-Uncle Sempronio!*

As for Great-Uncle Sempronio – to put your minds at ease, because I'm sure you have a soft spot for old people – I will tell you that, well, yes, he was dead, but it happened at the age of ninety-nine, after he'd enjoyed a long life with all his many millions, and having such an unpleasant great-nephew had never bothered him for a moment.

Everyone expected all of the dearly departed's wealth to pass into the hands of his sole heir, and that was indeed what the solicitor was saying as he read the will in his monotonous voice. In fact, his voice was so slow and boring that Alfonso, sure that he already knew how the story was going to end, had almost nodded off. But then a line of the will hit him like a cold shower, making him leap up out of the chair.

'Whaaat??!!' spluttered the young man, gaping and opening his eyes wide.

Patiently, the solicitor reread the last paragraph: '*My only great-nephew, Alfonso Terribile, will take possession of my entire fortune one year and one month after my death, on one condition: that by that date he has married a witch.*'

'But this is madness!' yelled Alfonso. 'It has to be a joke, right? A witch? What century are we living in? Even little children know there's no such thing as witches these days!'

'Please calm down, sir, and allow me to continue reading,' said the solicitor calmly, and he went back to reading the will. '*I am aware that my great-nephew will think this condition absurd and will claim that witches no longer exist. But they most certainly do exist. You just have to know how to recognise them. I am quite an expert in this matter, in fact, as I was very happily married to my Prunisinda for many years, and she was a true witch through and through.'*

'Great-Aunt Prunisinda was a witch?!' exclaimed Alfonso, who had only the vaguest memory of Great-Uncle Sempronio's wife, a chubby and cheerful woman who had passed away more than twenty years earlier.

'*We were so happy together, in fact,*' the solicitor continued reading, '*that I would like to ensure the same happiness for my heir. So he must put his wits to work. Find a young witch. Woo her and wed her. If he has not succeeded within one year and one month of my death, then he is out of luck. My fortune will pass to the person or persons who are mentioned inside this sealed envelope, which may not be opened until that date comes. Until then, the solicitor must keep the envelope in his safe.'*

'This is insane!' Alfonso puffed and panted,

feeling quite stunned. 'Find a witch? Woo a witch? Convince her to marry me?! But . . . that's impossible!'

However, Great-Uncle Sempronio's many millions – fifty of them, to be precise – were too tempting for him to give up just like that. Alfonso Terribile was going to do whatever it took to satisfy the conditions of his great-uncle's will.

BIOGRAPHY

Bianca Pitzorno was born in Sardinia, but has lived and worked in Milan, Italy, since 1968. She studied Classics and, after a brief period as an archaeologist and a teacher, she worked for many years for Rai, the Italian national public broadcasting company, producing a large number of television shows for children. Her first book was published in 1970, and she has since written more than fifty books, which have been translated into many languages. In 1996, the University of Bologna granted her an honorary degree in educational science, and UNICEF made her a Goodwill Ambassador in 2001.